TERRIBLE STORM

By Carol Otis Hurst

Pictures by S. D. Schindler

 GREENWILLOW BOOKS
An Imprint of HarperCollinsPublishers

AUTHOR'S NOTE

The Blizzard of 1888 was a devastating storm because of its length and severity, and because it was totally unexpected. It came in mid-March after a very warm winter, and the weather forecast predicted rain. Then the wind shifted and the snow began. The storm lasted three days and completely isolated most of New England and New York City.

At that time, the White Horse Tavern was a popular spot in Westfield, Massachusetts, and it was in the crowded lobby that Fred Clark, my shy grandfather, had to stay for the three days of the storm. The White Horse Tavern was also where my more sociable grandfather, Walter Otis, headed as soon as he freed himself from three days alone on his farm. When as old men they reminisced about the "terrible storm," it seemed that they agreed about how things had gone, but actually their reactions to the events had been almost totally opposite.

—Carol Otis Hurst

Terrible Storm
Text copyright © 2007 by Carol Otis Hurst
Illustrations copyright © 2007 by S. D. Schindler
All rights reserved. Manufactured in China.
www.harpercollinschildrens.com

Watercolors and black ink were used to prepare the full-color art.
The text type is Opti Adrift.

Library of Congress Cataloging-in-Publication Data
Hurst, Carol Otis.
Terrible storm / by Carol Otis Hurst; illustrations by S. D. Schindler.
p.   cm.
"Greenwillow Books."
Summary: A child's two grandfathers relate their boyhood experiences of the "terrible blizzard of 1888,"
during which each was stuck for three days doing what he disliked the most.
ISBN-10: 0-06-009001-4 (trade bdg.) ISBN-13: 978-0-06-009001-2 (trade bdg.)
ISBN-10: 0-06-009002-2 (lib. bdg.) ISBN-13: 978-0-06-009002-9 (lib. bdg.)
[1. Blizzards—Fiction. 2. Grandfathers—Fiction. 3. Individuality—Fiction.
4. Massachusetts—History—1865——Fiction.] I. Schindler, S. D., ill. II. Title.
Pz7.H95678 Ter 2007 [E]—dc22 2005035731

First Edition 10 9 8 7 6 5 4 3 2 1

 Greenwillow Books

To Keith and Jesse,
the great-great-grandsons of Walter and Fred
—C. O. H.

My grandfathers grew up in the hills around Westfield, Massachusetts, and were friends from the time they were boys.

Grandpa Otis (Walt) loved to be around people.

This was his idea of a good time.

Grandpa Clark (Fred) was a bit shy.

He was happiest like this.

When they were old men, they often sat on the porch together and talked about the "terrible storm," the Blizzard of 1888.

"Nice day."

"Yes sir."

"Not like March of '88, Fred."

"No sir!"

"Wasn't supposed to snow at all that day, Fred."

"No sir!"

"Clouds looked good that morning."

"Wind was from the west, Walt."

"And it was warm for March."

"Where were you when it hit?"

"Worse place I could have been."

"Me, too."

"I was drawing wood, wearing just a jacket and a cap."

"Delivering milk.
No boots or scarf."

"Began to snow about mid-morning, didn't it?"

"Eh-yah. Didn't think it would amount to much."

"By noon, it was thick on the ground."

"Ey-ah. Came quick when it came, all right."

"Still thought I could get my work done,

but the horse was nervous."

"Work kept getting harder and harder."

"Then the wind began to blow."

"Couldn't see where I was going."

"Had to take cover in the worst possible place."

"Was warm enough, of course."

"And out of the storm, at least."

"Had enough to eat."

"Not much of a place to sleep."

"Nothing to do."

"Sure wasn't what
I'd have chosen."

"Beggars can't be choosy, they say."

"Had to stay
there three whole days."

"An awful time."

"Thought I'd go crazy."

"Snow finally stopped
at noon on the third day."

"Had to dig my way out."

"Right! Dig and then lead
the horse."

"Yes sir! Then stop and dig some more."

"Tough on the hills."

"Things got better as I went."

"Passed you on the way, didn't I?"

"Everybody was in a hurry to get
where they were going."

"Right. Picked up speed
as I got closer."

"I'll tell you, I was mighty glad to see the place at last."

"Right where I belonged."

"Terrible storm, Fred."

"Worse one ever, Walt."